A FLYING DUCK

To order additional copies of this book, contact:
Xlibris
1-888-795-4274
www.Xlibris.com
Orders@Xlibris.com

ISBN: Softcover   978-1-7960-5220-6
         EBook   978-1-7960-5219-0

Print information available on the last page

Rev. date: 01/31/2020

To ALL the Good people on this planet

To ALL my Nieces and Nephews

Thank you ALL for making my life worth living

"But small is the gate and narrow the road that leads to life, and only a few find it" Matthew 7:14

GOD IS LOVE AND LIFE IS BEAUTIFUL

In puppy light years, in a town called Idan, where everything flies and the water is purple, the people have mingled with the animals and they are all supernatural breeds with supernatural powers.

The only animal that cannot fly is the Duck.

There is an old woman called Majustu-shi, who lives with the only Duck that can fly and this duck, produces, Diamond Eggs.

The Duck is so precious that Majustu-shi, cannot share it with anyone and cannot give it to anyone.

It has more power than all the kings and queens on the planet and as such, very many evil and bad men want to have this duck in their possession

They have meetings all the time, planning and strategizing when and how they will steal the

Duck from Majustu-shi, and every time they try, they cannot seem to find Majustu-shi or she has vanished and moved to another place to hide.

She got this duck from her ailing Grandfather called Maboroshino, who had guarded it for years as he knew the kind of power this Duck had.

The Duck is capable of turning into a crystal ball and show the owner what will happen more than 20 years to come.

When the Duck is happy, it can move mountains and create rain, where there was drought.

It can also, turn into a sculpture and when placed anywhere, can transform anyone in that room into a very happy person.

The Duck is capable of changing people into other forms or other people, when they are being followed by their enemies to camouflage them and make them invisible.

The Duck never ages and it has been on the planet for years. The only way to safe guard the duck is being owned by a good person, who will not misuse it for its powers.

And if a bad person gets it, the duck destroys them and causes havoc on their land and their family.

The other condition is that when a good person gets the Duck, they should keep it safe from harm and not give it to anyone, up until the duck becomes a crystal ball and shows the current owner of its next keeper.

It is a duty and a privilege to protect the Flying Duck. As it is the only one in the world and everyone wants it for themselves, so that they can use its powers to get riches.

Majustu-shi is always running, turning into different forms and animals just so she can protect the Duck. Sometimes she could be hiding in plain sight and her enemies would not even see her.

There is an evil king from another planet called Lakmi that has been watching her moves for a really long time, he has a bird called IdiBon, this bird has a power of camouflage, and it can see Majustu-shi from a far.

It has followed her and has learned when she turns, how she turns and where she hides.

Lakmi, prepares a number of his army to go and get the Flying Duck, they use IdiBon to trace her tracks and when she is out in the woods looking for fruits and vegetables to go cook, they sneak into her house, that was hidden in a cave and take the Flying Duck. They tie the Duck's feet and wings so that it does not fly as they are transporting it to Lakmi's Palace.

26

The army of 7 men is given strict instructions by Lakmi to make sure they each get to carry the duck, so that it does not have time to change and hurt the men before they deliver it to Lakmi. IdiBon must make a "caw caw" sound, if he feels the Duck is trying to get away so that the men can change possession of it.

The first horseman holds it and just as they are about to take off, there is a strong gush of wind that almost makes the men fall off their horses. IdiBon screaches "caw caw" and the first horseman throws the Duck to the next man. The minute the Duck is not in his possession, the wind comes strongly towards his direction, carrying him from his horse and throwing him far from the rest of the men into an endless pit.

And a strong female voice echoes throughout the forest, "Do not give the Flying Duck to anyone"

The horsemen are now scared and none of them even want to possess the Flying Duck as it is clear the kind of power the Duck has.

The second man holds it and beckons his horse to move faster to get back to Lakmi as fast as possible. Seconds later, the sky opens pouring boulders of rock and they come down on the forest hitting the men.

IdiBon, lets out a "caw caw" sound and the second man, quickly throws the Duck to the third horseman.

Seconds after he does this, the stones from the sky, fall on him and his horse, burying them under huge boulders of rock that the other men cannot move.

A voice from above comes again and says "Do not give the Flying Duck to anyone" "It only belongs to good people"

The remaining 5 men are now very scared and do not want to hold the duck or give it to anyone.

The third man holds the Duck and is frantically beckoning his horse to run as fast as he can so they can get back to Lakmi and they do not have to give or hold A Flying Duck.

Once he gets a hold of it, a bright burning light comes from above and burns the horsemen and you can see smoke coming from their heads and animals. The third horseman does not even hold the Duck for a few seconds he quickly releases it and takes off into the woods. The bright light, shines hard on him and his horse and right before the others eyes, he turns into flames, then amber, then dust and disappears.

Once again a loud voice from above says "Do not give the Flying Duck to anyone" "A Flying Duck is only good to good people"

"Caw Caw, Caw Caw" yells IdiBon, "caw caw caw"

The Fourth horseman, picks up the Flying Duck puts it on his lap and starts heading towards Lakmi's Palace; Just as he takes off, thunderstorm and Lightning hit the forest, Striking the 4th horseman right on his head, sending him to the floor leaving the Flying Duck on the horse. The Horse is so scared and tries to shake the Duck from his back. Heavy rain pours on the struck horseman that he drowns in his tracks.

Once again a voice comes from above "The Flying Duck is not for bad people, it is only for the Good" "Leave the Flying Duck alone and do not give it to anyone"

"Caw Caw Caw Caw Caw" Idibon yells, "Caw Caw Caw"

The fifth horseman rides to the fourth horseman's horse grabs the Duck in a frantic bid to take it to Lakmi so they can stop going through what they are going through.

As soon as he picks the Duck, balls of fire start flying down from above. Hot balls of fire; which, burn their spears and weapons. So hot that the Duck turns into a red hot ball of flame. The fifth horseman cannot hold the Duck as it is too hot, he lets go and in split second him and his horse turn into a ball of fire and disappears.

Once more the voice from above louder than ever says "You cannot handle a Flying Duck" "Do not give the Flying Duck to people who are not good"

This time IdiBon, is so scared that he has flown fast to Lakmi to beg him not to take or give a Flying Duck, but Lakmi does not want to listen to his smart camouflage bird.

The remaining 2 horsemen are sweating and do not want anything to do with the Flying Duck.

Their faces had turned into beads of water, their eyes wide open and their hands trembling like shaking leaves.

They knew they had to accomplish the task of Taking the Flying Duck and Giving it – but they were too scared to handle how much Power lay in Giving a Flying Duck. They had to complete Lakmi's work as they worked for him.

They listened to the voice from above that echoed
"You can only give a Flying Duck to a good person"
"Do not give a Flying Duck to Lakmi"

The 6th Horseman, with many doubts, took the Duck, put it under his arms and headed straight to Lakmi's Palace. The 7th horseman called onto him telling him they should return the Flying Duck to Majustu-shi, but the 6th horseman was determined to take the Duck to Lakmi and share in its riches. Just as the horse took the second gallop, arrows of Ice, came falling down from the skies, so sharp that they pierced the horseman's shoes and pinned him down to the ground. The horse took off leaving the horseman covered with ice picks.

This time, there was no "caw caw" from IdiBon and the last horseman was all on his own.

Back at the palace all the things that had attacked the horsemen from above had attacked Lakmi and his palace and IdiBon kept begging Lakmi to give him the order to go and let the 7th horseman to take back the Flying Duck to Majustu-shi. But Lakmi did not want to hear any of it and threw a bottle towards IdiBon, breaking his neck and leaving him lying on the floor.

The 7th horseman, went and picked the Flying Duck, looked above and the skies opened to a beautiful wonderful sun and a rainbow filled with magical colors appeared.

The voice from above whispered "The Flying Duck belongs only to good people"

He kissed the duck and turned his horse back to Majustu-shi's house

His path was opened like an enchanted red carpet, the birds, animals and environment sang sweet songs.

He was the best of the 7 horsemen, he decided that his job was not to hurt but to protect good people and he listened to the voice from above.

He got to Majustu-shi's house and found her waiting for him with a buffet of great food for him to partake.

Animals had lined up at his arrival and he was treated like a Hero.

The Flying Duck lay 3 Diamond Eggs when he held it and smiled at him. He knew he had received blessing because he was the only one who had given a Flying Duck to good people.

Majustu-shi dined with the 7th Horseman, took off his coat and his boots to reveal bracelets on his wrists and his ankles, and she smiled broadly, telling him she had been waiting for him.

She asked "What is your name son", and he said....

My name is M. "Well", she said in an old frail voice – "M, the Flying Duck is yours to keep and protect good people with".

Song

Pluck Pluck
Is that your Duck? Cluck Cluck
It's not my Duck
Quack Quack It's all for Luck Quack Quack
A Great Flying Duck
Quack Quack
How good it is to give a Flying Duck

A Flying Duck

Stephine Ngutah and Rachel Jael

Printed in the United States
By Bookmasters